HARRIET ZIEFERT

I Swapped My Dog

Illustrated by Emily Bolam

HOUGHTON MIFFLIN COMPANY BOSTON

1 9 9 8

For my unswappable family
HMZ

Walter Lorraine (wr) Books

Copyright © 1998 by Harriet Ziefert

All rights reserved. For information about permission
to reproduce selections from this book, write to
Permissions, Houghton Mifflin Company, 215 Park
Avenue South, New York, New York 10003.

Library of Congress Cataloging-in-Publication Data
Ziefert, Harriet.
   I swapped my dog / by Harriet Ziefert ; illustrated by Emily
Bolam.
      p. cm.
   Summary: A farmer makes a series of trades and ends up with the
dog he had at the start.
   ISBN 0-395-89159-0
   [1. Animals—Fiction. 2. Stories in rhyme.] I. Bolam, Emily,
ill. II. Title.
PZ8.3.Z49Iaak   1998   97-29430
[E]—dc21   CIP
                                                        AC

Printed in China for Harriet Ziefert Inc.
HZI 10 9 8 7 6 5 4 3 2 1

I had a dog
He'd run by my side.

But I wanted an animal
That I could ride.

I swapped my dog
And I got me a mare.

She kicked and she neighed
And she threw me in the air!

I swapped my mare
And got me a mule.

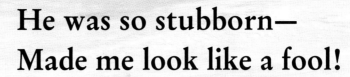

He was so stubborn—
Made me look like a fool!

I swapped my mule
And got me a goat.

I swapped my goat
And got me a sheep.
She baa'd so loud
I couldn't sleep!

I swapped my sheep
And got me a cow.

I tried to get milk
But I didn't know how!

I swapped my cow
And got me a pig.

All he ever did
Was grunt and dig!

I swapped my pig
And got me a hen.

She wouldn't lay eggs.
Know what I did then?

I swapped my hen
And got me a cat.

Darned old cat
Was scared of a rat!

After all that swapping
I did decide…

What I really wanted
Was a dog by my side.

My old black dog
He's my best friend.
We'll stay together
Until the end!